HENRI MOUSE

THE JUGGLER

STORY BY
GEORGE MENDOZA

PICTURES BY
JOELLE BOUCHER

VIKING KESTREL

VIKING KESTREL
Viking Penguin Inc., 40 West 23rd Street, New York, New York 10010, U.S.A.
Penguin Books Ltd, Harmondsworth, Middlesex, England
Penguin Books Australia Ltd, Ringwood, Victoria, Australia
Penguin Books Canada Limited, 2801 John Street, Markham, Ontario, Canada L3R 1B4
Penguin Books (N.Z.) Ltd, 182–190 Wairau Road, Auckland 10, New Zealand

First published in 1986 by Viking Penguin Inc.
Published simultaneously in Canada

Printed in Japan by Dai Nippon. Set in Korinna.
1   2   3   4   5   90   89   88   87   86

Library of Congress Cataloging in Publication Data
Mendoza, George.   Henri Mouse, juggler.
Summary: Henri Mouse becomes a world-famous juggler with
magical powers when he chances upon a special juggler's ball.
[1. Mice—Fiction.   2. Jugglers and juggling—Fiction]
I. Boucher, Joelle, ill.   II. Title.
PZ7.M5255Hde   1986   [E]   85-20186   ISBN 0-670-80945-4

For Michael David Sekora

G.M.

Pour mes amis
Raymond Wapner et Pierre Courmont

J.B.

After his splendid career as an artist in Paris, Henri Mouse turned to street juggling. This came about quite by accident, while he was working on what was to be his last painting.

You may recall that Henri had a special talent; everything he painted disappeared. And so, when Henri Mouse sat in his favorite café and drew a street juggler's ball, an ordinary red ball about the size of a grapefruit, you can imagine the scene that followed.

There was the street juggler searching frantically for his missing ball. And there was Henri Mouse walking away with it, totally unaware that he had captured the ball on the canvas tucked under his arm.

As he made his way home, Henri Mouse could hear the street juggler crying over and over, *"My ball! Someone stole my ball!"*

Another crazy person, Henri Mouse thought in an absentminded way.

When he got home, Henri propped his painting on the edge of the bathtub so he could admire it while he took a bath.

Turning on the tap, Henri went into his bedroom to get undressed. When he

returned to the bathroom, he discovered to his great surprise that his painting had slipped into the tub. The picture had washed away, but now a red ball was floating on the water.

"Cat's whiskers!" said Henri. "What is this?"

Henri Mouse threw the ball into the air. To his amazement little stars sparkled all around it. And then, to his greater amazement, he saw himself inside the ball dressed as a magician.

"Cat's cradle! Just like a crystal ball!" Henri cried out, startled. "What's going on here?"

Henri threw the ball up again. This time the ball made a loud, popping sound and suddenly became two balls.

Henri couldn't believe what he was seeing now. For inside one ball he appeared as a matador, while in the other he was a cowboy on a rearing stallion.

Then, as the balls came down, they became one bright red ball again.

Henri jumped up and down and laughed with delight. "Magic," he sang, "I've found a magic ball."

It was at that very moment that Henri Mouse decided to go out into the streets of Paris and become a magical juggler extraordinaire.

Children by the hundreds and thousands followed Henri Mouse, the magical juggler, all over Paris. Mothers and fathers, grandmothers and grandfathers, young people in love, cats and dogs, and even pigeons from faraway roosts followed Henri to watch his wondrous juggling act.

Of course, Henri no longer looked like he did when he was an artist. In place of his beret, he wore a shiny top hat; in place of his artist's cape a very formal magician's black coat with tails.

Henri could perform miracles with his magic ball. In fact, he never knew what to expect when he threw his ball into the air. For each time there was another surprise.

Sometimes the red ball became one, two, three, four balls, each with its own magical scene inside.

Sometimes Henri had to juggle twenty balls at a time—balls filled with fish, roosters, dogs, dancing pigs, owls, and frogs, juggling them up and down, faster and faster. Even though he grew dizzy, juggling furiously with his hands, feet, nose, elbows, and knees, he never, never let a single ball touch the ground. And all the time the children were laughing and looking, pointing and shouting, ''More, Henri! More!''

Once his magic red ball multiplied itself into a rainbow of juggling balls that exploded and filled the sky with a showery burst of fireworks, a spectacular sight for all Paris to see!

While Henri Mouse was becoming the most famous mouse juggler in the world, he was also becoming a very, very rich mouse. Soon he had to move into a mansion large enough to store all the money he had received from his admirers.

He was so famous now, he needed ferocious bodyguards around him at all times:
four huge cats with claws as long as pitchforks and fangs as sharp as a saber-toothed
tiger's teeth.

He was asked to perform for kings and queens and presidents of faraway lands and
even for the Pope in the Vatican!

One evening Henri Mouse discovered that something new and strange was happening to his magic ball. It wasn't turning into balls anymore. It was turning into EGGS!

And during other performances the magic ball turned into—
fish,
stars,

shells,
marbles,
toys,

masks,

dolls,

oranges,

pears, prunes, grapes,

bread, rolls, bread sticks, pastries,

and on one occasion, feathers!

Feathers, as Henri discovered, were the most difficult to juggle since he had to blow on each one to keep it in the air. But he did it!

Then one day something very strange happened to the red ball. When Henri threw it up into the sky, it hung over the city instead of coming down. Everyone could see that it was growing bigger and bigger with each passing second, until you couldn't see the sun, you couldn't see the clouds, you couldn't see anything but a gigantic, round, red balloon that almost blotted out the sky.

"It's going to burst!" shouted some onlookers.

"It's the juggler's fault!" yelled others.

"Stop! Please stop!" cried Henri. And suddenly there was a great *whoosh*, and a frenzied whirlwind blew all over Paris. Henri was amazed to find the red ball back in his hands again, but before he could catch his breath, he found himself being pulled off

the ground, pulled higher and higher by the magic ball.

"Cat's nine lives!" cried Henri Mouse. "Don't drop me, please!" Squeezing his eyes shut, he held onto the ball for dear life.

Suddenly Henri found himself standing inside a gondola that swayed beneath a marvelous huge balloon.

"You certainly are full of surprises," he exclaimed. And then, from far below, he heard a familiar voice crying in the street: *"My ball! Someone stole my ball!"*

It was the poor street juggler, still looking for his ball.

Henri noticed a small, ordinary red ball rolling across the gondola floor. "I have new adventures before me," he thought, "wherever they are, whatever they may be." And he picked up the ball and dropped it over the side back to earth.

As the balloon began to lift, catching the stronger air currents, Henri Mouse thought he heard a very distant, faraway "thank you," but he wasn't sure.